I'm Going to Run Away

Words and Pictures by
Joan Hanson

Platt & Munk Publishers/New York

A Division of Grosset & Dunlap

They never let me do anything around here.

When I take a bath they won't let me have any fun.

And I have to wash my hands before I eat.

I can't even go barefoot, for goodness' sake.

It's so stupid around here.
I'm going to pack my suitcase and run away.
Let's see, what shall I take?

I'll need to take my favorite pajamas with the feet in them—
and probably my bed, too.
Hmmm . . . this is too small.
I'll have to take a bigger bag.

I'll take the icicles I've been saving in the freezer
and a jar of peanut butter
and some bubble gum—
I'm bound to get hungry while I'm gone.
I think I'll bring my boots in case it rains—
but not the one that leaks.

And my new sneakers.
And if I take those
I'll need my father to tie my shoelaces.

And I'd better take my brother
so I'll have someone to fight with.
I'll pack my collection of bugs and worms
(they like to travel).

And perhaps my special apple tree
with the swing in it.

Then there's my sharp stick.
If I meet a monster on the road I'll poke him.
And I'll need my batman costume that my mother made—
and my mother—
who else would kiss me good night?

I'm not running away from home.
I'm taking it with me.

I think I'll stay here.
It's easier.

Besides—I smell cookies baking in the kitchen.
And tomorrow I have to shampoo the gerbils,
move my sandpile into the house,
take my toads out of the desk drawer. . . .